ISBN: 9798555782137

To Sophie
Love you to the moon and back
Auntie Nicky and Brian
xxx

Acknowledgements

Having spent nearly twenty years working with children and young people, books and stories have played a huge part in all aspects of my career. From sharing stories in nurseries, to researching lessons as a lecturer, to studying the way that books are created in my degree. Books are such special things, they have a magical ability to allow us to lose ourselves in their pages, to feel like we are at one with the characters and find resolution in their storylines. My love of books has been one which spans years, and some of my favourites still sit on my book shelf. In 2014 I left my full-time teaching post and told my tutor group that I would dedicate my time to developing my book collection, which had sat as an idea in notebooks for so long. On the arrival of Brian, my real-life cockapoo, in 2015 the dream just became more and more real. I am delighted to be able to share the Adventures of Brian with families and bring the magic of books and the wonders of therapeutic storytelling together to offer a combination of stories and support to children. Before we start this special story, there is thanks to be given;

To my Mum and Dad, who have given me the encouragement to move forward with a dream of creating stories to help small people. Thank you for standing by me, encouraging me and sharing these precious moments.

To Richard for your belief and encouragement that there was a set of books inside me that should be written, this shiny diamond is very grateful.

To my nan and grandad, who forever guide me to follow this path that I am on and to ensure that I stay true to my dreams.

To Veronica and Brian, eternally in my heart, you inspired the little fluffy boy who became the centre of these books and shared so many precious memories.

A big congratulations to Arabella for winning our 'design a character' competition during lockdown, Millie the monkey is a welcomed new character in this book.

Finally, to all our friends who have supported us, encouraged us and inspired us in the development of the Adventures of Brian, we are so grateful for your love each and every day.

I hope you enjoy these books as much as I have enjoyed writing them

Love Nicky x x

THE ADVENTURES OF BRIAN

HELPING CHILDREN OVERCOME THEIR FEARS AND WORRIES

This book belongs to:

....

Brian sat in the car and looked out of the window. He loved a trip out in the car with his mummy. Today he was going on a special day out with his nanny and grandad – his mummy was coming too!

As they drove along, Brian wondered where they were going. He was very excited but a little bit worried, as he was not sure what to expect. He could feel the worried feeling in his tummy spinning round and round. He took a big breath and instead looked out of the car window at the trees, trying to spot squirrels.

Finally, grandad slowed down and parked the car. Brian was eager to get out, he squealed in excitement to remind his mummy to get him out too!

As soon as he was out of the car, he sniffed the air and looked around to try and work out where they were.

Brian looked around, there were lots of trees and colours. In front of them was a huge building that said 'welcome' over the door. He could not work it out. There were lots of people though!

Brian looked at all the legs and felt the worried feeling in his tummy grow bigger. He nudged his mummy with his nose and she picked him up. He much preferred it high up where he could see what was happening.

His mummy pointed at the sign, "are you ready Brian?" she asked. Brian hid in her hair, he did not know what he was meant to be ready for?

As they walked towards the big sign, Brian saw pictures of lots of animals, he knew some of them, but was not sure about the rest. His mummy stopped to show him. "This is a wildlife park Brian" she told him. He listened carefully, "all the animals were rescued to help them to safety" she explained.

Brian thought about the rescue dogs he met and the rescue centre he gave gifts to at Christmas and began to understand. He wondered who they would see...

As they walked around Brian darted back and forth, there was so much to look at he was not sure which way to go! There were people and animals, and more people and more animals. The swirling in his tummy was getting bigger and he felt a bit tearful.

He looked around at his mummy and she scooped him up in a big hug. There was just too much to look at, he did not know what to do!

His mummy fluffed his head as she asked, "are you feeling a bit overwhelmed Brian?". Brian was not sure what an overwhelm was? Maybe it was this funny feeling he had that just made him want to cry even though it was such a nice day? He needed to ask Blue Butterfly.

As they walked around the next bend, Brian noticed something brown fly through the air, it scared him so much he barked and then hid under his mummy's arm.

Brian's mummy held him up so he could see, there in the tree in front of them was a little monkey, with the biggest brown eyes that Brian had ever seen. He stretched to look a little closer and the monkey reached her hand out towards him.

"Hi, you scared me!" Brian told her. The monkey smiled, "sorry!" she replied. Brian grinned, now he could see her she was not scary, in fact he thought she was very cute.

"My name is Millie" she told him. "I'm Brian!" he replied.

Brian wiggled to get down from his mummy's arms and wandered closer to Millie. She hopped down from her tree and came to see him. Brian was a little bit excited now, and his little tail wagged ever so fast.

Millie looked closely at Brian, "why were you so upset?" she asked. Brian dropped his head and looked at the floor. "I keep getting this swirly feeling in my tummy, and it gets so big it makes me want to cry" he told her.

Millie listened carefully, nodding as he spoke. "What made it happen?" she asked. Brian looked all around them, "it's all these people, and colours and animals….there is just so much to take in" he whispered.

Millie nodded again, "I get a feeling like that sometimes" she told him.

Brian's eyes became wider, he thought it was just him! "How do you manage it?" he asked her.

Millie sat down, so Brian sat down too so he could listen carefully. "Well Brian, I find a safe place to sit until the feeling gets smaller, and sometimes I ask the other monkey's if they can help me make it better" she told him.

Brian thought that Millie's ideas were very good. When he got the feeling, he liked to be picked up by his mummy as he knew that he was safe. He also preferred to be somewhere quiet and peaceful as it let the swirling slow down.

"It's not a nice feeling, is it?" he replied.

Millie shook her head. "No, it's a horrid feeling Brian, it makes me want to cry and I don't like how it feels inside my body" she told him.

"Does it ever make you angry?" Brian asked.

Millie nodded, "yes, sometimes I get really cross as the feeling is so big and I cannot make it smaller. Sometimes I scream or get angry as it scares me" she told him.

Brian was so glad that he was not the only one with the feeling. It made him feel better to talk about it.

As they said their goodbyes, Brian hoped that he would meet Millie again one day, it was lovely to have a new friend who understood him so much.

When they arrived home, Brian was so tired, but he ran into the garden in hope that he might find Blue Butterfly. As he ran across the grass she was just floating down into the flowers.

"Blue Butterfly! Blue Butterfly!" Brian cried, running towards her! "Brian! I've missed you!" she replied. Brian grinned, he really did love Blue Butterfly.

He settled down next to her flower and told her all about his day, and meeting Millie the Monkey. Blue Butterfly listened carefully to everything he had to say.

Brian explained about the swirling feeling in his tummy and how it had made him sad and angry. Blue Butterfly nodded, "it sounds like it was a bit overwhelming" she replied. Brian looked up, "what does overwhelming mean?" he asked her.

Blue Butterfly wriggled on her flower and explained, "sometimes, when we do things it can make our feelings really big and strong. It's like they take over and we cannot control them" she told him.

Brian nodded, this is EXACTLY how he felt! His swirling was so big it made him cry, it was a huge feeling! "How do I stop it?" he asked Blue Butterfly.

Blue Butterfly smiled, well he thinks she did, it was hard to tell. "Brian, the first thing you can do, is take a big breath and find a space where it is quieter and safe to take a rest in. You must make sure an adult is there though".

Brian thought about this, finding a quiet spot would help, as then he could look and see what was happening. It was very hard to take everything in when there were so many people and animals everywhere!

"I think that would help" he told her. "There were so many colours, people and animals I did not know where to look" he explained to Blue Butterfly.

Blue Butterfly nodded, "when we are somewhere busy or new it can quickly become overwhelming. If you find a quiet space you can look at where everything is, and then you can make a plan. Taking time to look really helps" she explained.

Brian wishes he had done that, he thought about what Millie had said about finding a safe place, this was what she meant!

Brian looked at Blue Butterfly, "is there anything else I can do?" he asked.

Blue Butterfly nodded again, "well Brian, you should always tell an adult that your feelings are overwhelming, then they can help you too. They might be able to help you find ideas of how to make it better".

Brian thought about this, if he told his mummy, or nanny and grandad, that the feelings were overwhelming, he knew that they would make a plan to help make it better.

He grinned at Blue Butterfly, "thank you Blue Butterfly, you always have such good ideas" he told her. He gave her a little kiss and she floated up into the sky, "see you soon Brian!" she called.

The next weekend, Brian's mummy took him to the forest for a walk, he loved the leaves and the colours, but when they got near the lake it was busy and he felt the swirling feeling coming back again.

Brian thought about what Blue Butterfly had said, and he looked at his mummy and tugged her towards a quiet spot. They sat on the bench together and Brian looked all around them.

Brian could see the people, the lake and the trees. There were ducks on the lake and dogs running around.

He snuggled into his mummy and she talked about what they could see. Slowly, Brian noticed that the swirling feeling was calming down and the tears were disappearing.

Taking a moment to sit in a safe place really did help!

Once the feeling was back under control, Brian noticed that there was a lot of wonderful things to see.

Brian looked all around and decided that first he wanted to see the ducks, so he hopped off the bench and dragged his mummy down towards the water where he sat and watched the ducks float across the lake. He made sure to notice everything so he could tell Millie all about them when he next saw her.

From that day forward, Brian always remembered, that if his feelings became overwhelming he needed to find a safe, quiet space with an adult and take a moment to let things calm down. Then he could make a plan so things were easier.

So, Brian was able to enjoy more adventures and have more fun than ever before, because now he knew how to calm down the big feelings.

THE ADVENTURES

OF BRIAN

HELPING CHILDREN OVERCOME THEIR FEARS AND WORRIES

Other books in this series:

Nicky lives in Sussex with Brian the Cockapoo where they enjoy daily adventures with friends and family. Nicky started her career by spending 10 years working in the early years sector with 0-5 year olds before lecturing in early years and health and social care to students aged 16 and over. She later retrained as a hypnotherapist and now runs A Step at a Time Hypnotherapy working with children and adults to resolve their personal issues.

The Adventures of Brian books were the development of a dream of wanting to offer parents of young children tools and resources to support their children to manage worries and fears in a non-intrusive way. Having spent a large part of her career reading stories at all speeds and in all voices this collection of storybooks was born.

Each book in the collection covers a different worry which affects children on a day to day basis and uses therapeutic storytelling to support children in resolving these through Brian's daily adventures.

You can find more titles in the Adventures of Brian series by visiting:

www.adventuresofbrian.co.uk

Printed in Great Britain
by Amazon